C. M. Velazquez

STRANGERS IN THE NIGHT

Printed in the United States of America

Library of Congress Control Number:		2022921801
ISBN:	Softcover	979-8-88622-815-1
	e-Book	979-8-88622-816-8

Republished by: PageTurner Press and Media LLC
Publication Date: 12/06/2022

To order copies of this book, contact:
PageTurner Press and Media
Phone: 1-888-447-9651
info@pageturner.us
www.pageturner.us

It was a sunny day. Eleven year-old Jonathan was riding his bike, on the way home from school. Jonathan was a boy who loved to visit his friends while on his way home.

He saw Brian. Brian was in his garage. "Hey, Brian what are you doing?" shouted Jonathan. "Oh, I'm looking for my baseball mitt and I can't find it", Brian responded. "Want me to help you look for it, Jonathan?" said Jonathan. "Okay", said Brian.

Jonathan got off the bike and began helping Brian look for his baseball glove. The boys look tirelessly for the glove. They began looking in his mother's room but nothing, sister's room nothing. "Well, I don't think it would be in my brother's room", exclaimed Brian. "Why not?", asked Jonathan. "Okay, here nothing", said Brian.

The boys opened the door to Randall's room and to their surprise, Randall was lying in his bed covered from head to toe. Randall was home. Brian quickly ran towards his big brother, shaking him awake and said, "What are you doing home? You're supposed to be...,"."Oh leave me alone, get out of my room", shouted Randall. "But, you're supposed to be in school, not home sleeping. If mom and dad see you here, they'll be really angry with you," said Brian. "What happened Randall, tell me."

Brian and Jonathan sat down, at the edge of the bed waiting anxiously for explanation, forgetting the reason why they came into Randall's room. "Well I'll tell you, but, you promise not to tell mom and dad, I want to tell them myself. Promise?" said Randall. "Promise!", shouted both boys in unison.

13

It happened while on my way to school. I was driving on highway 12 and it was really cold, breezy and dark. I had on my high beams, but it wasn't doing much good. So, I decided to stop and rest for a while until I felt ready to drive again. So, while sitting alongside the highway a car stopped. I panicked a little, not sure what to expect." said Randall. Jonathan and Brian listened attentively. "This lady came out of the car, she looked very sophisticated. I was somewhat in a trance. I eyeball her from top of her head, to bottom of her feet. She was wearing black high heels shoes, black fitted dress and a red like, Goldilocks coat. Yeah, that's it." Randall became animated as he described the lady in goldilocks coat.

"I saw her, walking towards the car, she knocked on the window and asked me 'say are you alright, do you need any help? I looked up at her, not sure what to say, "Oh i'm fine, just that at night I can't see very well. So she gave me a smirk look and said, "so, you're going to stay here until day break", exclaimed the lady. "Oh no, I'm just resting my eyes." as I responded. "Oh come on, follow me, I will lead you to your destination. So I followed" as the lady responded, stammered Randall, as he talked of his venture on the road.

"What happened Randall, you followed her and then what?" Brian asked impatiently. "Ok let me finish. Yes, I followed her, but it wasn't where I thought it would lead me. It was this pool room, you know a hang out spot. Oh, Brian I know you're looking at me like such a fool. But it was the best thing at the time I could do. I couldn't see at night, I was all alone, what was I to do. I told the lady, "This isn't where I was heading." and "I know," said the lady. She mentioned, "Stay only for a little while."

So, I followed her in. I stayed for maybe a little over an hour, when I decided to leave, the lady came rushing towards me, grabbed at my arm and asked, "Where are you going?". "Home!" I yelled. And I walked away, not ever looking back. While driving for almost 20 minutes, I noticed that my car appeared to be shifting.

I got out of the car to check. To my surprise the tires were flat. I looked in the trunk. My bags were gone, the ones with all my ID's." "Wow, how can you be so..., " yelled Brian. "I know, I know, there's no need to beat me over the head, you see I can't tell mom and dad all of what happened, they will look at me the same idiotic way. It was when I decided to turn back and come home, no ID no bags. It is why I am at home trying to figure out how to explain this to them." said Randall.

"Well, exclaimed Jonathan, better be going home too. I've been out of school for, oh, let's see half an hour and no need to get my parents all worked up. Brian and I will see you tomorrow and maybe you'll have luck with finding that glove of yours", said Randall. "Oh yeah, I forgot about that." said Jonathan. "See you tomorrow Jonathan, Oh and thanks." said Randall.

Just then Brian and Randall's parents were walking in. "Hello" said his mother, giving Brian a peck on the cheek. "How was your day at school?" as their mom asked. "Oh it was fun. I did not have much school work today. Hi, dad!", said Brian. His dad responded, "Hello son, have you heard from your brother, he was supposed to call as soon as he gets to school." Brian responded, "Oh, no dad not yet." "Well when he does, call me as soon as he calls", said his dad. "Alright dad", yelled Brian back as he walked towards his mother.

In a soft whisper, Brian reached up towards his mother, as she crouched towards Brian looking at him peculiarly. "Mom, can I tell you something?" asked Brian. "Brian you know you can tell me anything", as mother responded. "Randall's upstairs", said Brian. "What?!", exclaimed his mother. Brian began to explain. "I'm going right up", said his mother. As she marched up the stairs, Brian shouted, "don't be too harsh on him, there's a reason for all of this".

As Ms. Thomas headed up the stairs, she could not help but give Randall a big hug so tightly, he didn't know what to make of it. "Are you alright? You're not hurt?" his mom worriedly asked. "No mother, not at all. I thank God for being alive", said Randall.

Randall's dad was standing by the doorway when he heard what had happened. He, too, gave Randall a hug. "So I'm just glad you're alive and well. But, you learn from mistakes. I do hope you learned yours. Don't wait for darkness to settle and then decide to leave. Leave when it is still daylight so you're able to see where you're going", explained Mr. Thomas. "I know dad, I just don't know why I believed this lady. She seemed friendly, innocent and helpful that I believed her. Boy, that really taught me a lesson", shouted Randall.

"Don't stop for strangers even if they are young and beautiful", Randall added. "Oh, so that was it son, you followed her beauty". Mr. & Mrs. Thomas chuckled. They hugged the boys with so much warmth they did not want to let go.

33

The End.